The Nursery Collection

Shirley Hughes

WALKER BOOKS
LONDON

First published individually as
Bathwater's Hot, When We Went to the Park,
Noisy (1985), and *Colours*
and *All Shapes and Sizes* (1986)
by Walker Books Ltd
87 Vauxhall Walk, London SE11 5HJ

This edition published 1994

2 4 6 8 10 9 7 5 3 1

This book has been typeset in Sabon.

Printed in Italy

British Library Cataloguing in Publication Data
A catalogue record for this book is
available from the British Library.

ISBN 0-7445-3210-8

Contents

Bathwater's Hot

Bathwater's hot,

Seawater's cold;

Ginger's kittens are *very* young,

But Buster's getting old.

Some things
you can
throw away,

Some are nice to keep;

Here's someone
who is wide awake...

Shhh, he's fast asleep!

Some things are hard as stone,
Some are soft as cloud;

Whisper very
quietly,

Shout
OUT LOUD!

14

It's fun to run
very fast,

Or to be slow;

The red light
says "stop",

And the green
light says "go".

It's kind to be helpful,

Unkind to tease;

Rather rude to push and grab,

Polite to say "please".

Night-time is dark,   Daytime is light;

The sun says
"good morning",

And the moon
says "good night".

Good night !

When We Went
to the Park

When Grandpa and I put on our coats and went to the park...

We saw one black cat sitting on a wall,

Two big girls licking ice-creams,

Three ladies chatting on a bench,

Four babies in buggies,

Five children playing in the sandpit,

Six runners running,

Seven dogs chasing one another,

Eight boys kicking a ball,

Nine ducks swimming on the pond,

Ten birds swooping
in the sky,

And so many leaves that
I couldn't count them all.

On the way back we saw
the black cat again.

Then we went home for tea.

Colours

Baby blues, navy blues,
Blue socks, blue shoes;

Blue plate, blue mug,
Blue flowers in a blue jug;

And fluffy white clouds floating by
In a great big beautiful bright blue sky.

Syrup dripping from a spoon,
Buttercups, a harvest moon;
Sun like honey on the floor,
Warm as the steps by our back door.

Scarlet leaves, bright berries,
Rosy apples, dark cherries;
And when the winter's day is done,
A fiery sky, a big red sun.

Tangerines and apricots,
Orange flowers in orange pots;
Orange glow on an orange mat,
Marmalade toast and a marmalade cat.

Berries in the bramble patch,
Pick them (but mind the thorns don't scratch)!
Purple blossom, pale and dark,
Spreading with springtime in the park.

Green lettuce, green peas,
Green shade from green trees;
And grass as far as you can see,
Like green waves in a green sea.

Shiny boots, a witch's hat,
Black cloak, black cat;
Black crows cawing high,
Winter trees against the sky.

Thistledown like white fluff,
Dandelion clocks to puff;
White snowflakes whirling down,
Covering gardens, roofs and town.

All Shapes and Sizes

Boxes have flat sides,
Balls are round;

High is
far up in
the sky,

Low is
near the
ground.

Some of us are rather short,
Some are tall;

Some pets are large, some are small.

Our cat's very fat,   Next door's is thin;

Big Teddy's out,   Little Teddy's in.

Squeeze through narrow spaces,

Run through wide;

Climb up the ladder,

Slip down the slide.

Get behind to push,

Get in front
to pull;

This
jar's
empty,

Now
it's
full.

48

Hats can be
many sizes,

So can feet;

Children of all ages playing in the street.

I can stand up
very straight,

Or I can
bend.

Here's a beginning,

And this is the end!

Noisy

Noisy noises! Pan lids clashing,

Dog barking, plate smashing;

Telephone ringing, baby bawling,
Midnight cats cat-a-wauling.

Door slamming,
Aeroplane zooming,

Vacuum cleaner
Vroom-vroom-
vrooming;

And if I dance
and sing a tune,
Baby joins in
with a saucepan
and spoon.

Gentle noises: dry leaves swishing,

Falling rain, splashing, splishing;

Rustling trees, hardly stirring,
Lazy cat softly purring.

Story's over,
Bedtime's come,

Crooning baby
Sucks his thumb;

All quiet, not a peep –
Everyone is fast asleep.